ideals
COUNTRY

SO-AZY-730

Vol. 47, No. 4

Publisher, Patricia A. Pingry
Associate Editor, Nancy Skarmeas
Photography and Permissions Editor,
Kathleen Gilbert
Contributing Editor, Bonnie Aeschliman
Art Director, Patrick McRae
Editorial Assistant, Fran Morley

ISBN 0-8249-1083-4

IDEALS—Vol. 47, No. 4 June MCMXC IDEALS (ISSN 0019-137X) is published eight times a year: February, March, May, June, August, September, November, December by IDEALS PUBLISHING CORPORATION, Nelson Place at Elm Hill Pike, Nashville, Tenn. 37214. Second-class postage paid at Nashville, Tennessee, and additional mailing offices. Copyright © MCMXC by IDEALS PUBLISHING CORPORATION. POSTMASTER: Send address changes to Ideals, Post Office Box 148000, Nashville, Tenn. 37214-8000. All rights reserved. Title IDEALS registered U.S. Patent Office.

SINGLE ISSUE—$4.95
ONE-YEAR SUBSCRIPTION—eight consecutive issues as published—$19.95
TWO-YEAR SUBSCRIPTION—sixteen consecutive issues as published—$35.95
Outside U.S.A., add $6.00 per subscription year for postage and handling.

ACKNOWLEDGMENTS

DADDIES from THE PATH TO HOME by Edgar A. Guest. Copyright 1919 by The Reilly & Lee Co. Used by permission of the Estate; THE FARMER from BESIDE STILL WATERS by Edna Jaques. Used by permission of Thomas Allen & Son Limited, CANADA; BUTTERFLIES from WHERE VIOLETS GROW by Ann Thompson Jester, Banner Press, Birmingham, Alabama; THE THINGS OF OTHER DAYS from COME ON HOME by Douglas Malloch. Copyright 1923 by George H. Doran Company. Used by permission of the Estate; VISITORS IN MY GARDEN from BLENDED THOUGHTS by Mamie Ozburn Odum. Used by permission; MEADOW MUSIC and I WOULDN'T TRADE from MOMENTS OF SUNSHINE, Copyright © 1974 by Garnett Ann Schultz. Used by permission; RIVERSIDE REVERIES from PATHS OF PROMISE by Patience Strong. Used by permission of Rupert Crew Limited, London, ENGLAND. Our sincere thanks to the following whose addresses we were unable to locate: the Estate of Joy Belle Burgess for AT DUSK; C.H. Channing for COUNTRY CHILD; Rosaline Guingrich for RURAL FULFILLMENT from HOMESPUN. Copyright 1971; Edna Greene Hines for GOD'S LINES from HARP OF THE PINES; the Estate of Roy Z. Kemp for GOD'S HELPER; Lon Myruski for DADDY'S FARM; Milly Walton for SUMMER SANCTUARY and ROADS from SOME SMALL DELIGHT. Copyright 1949 by Milly Walton.

Four-color separations by Rayson Films, Inc., Waukesha, Wisconsin

Printing by Ringier-America, Brookfield, Wisconsin

The paper used in this publication meets the minimum requirements of American National Standard for Information Sciences—Permanence of Paper for Printed Library Materials, ANSI Z39.48-1984.

Cover
The Old Mill of Pigeon Forge
Tennessee
b Clemenz Landscape Photography

Photo Opposite
Woodland Park Zoo
Seattle, Washington
Adam Jones, Photographer

I Wouldn't Trade

Garnett Ann Schultz

I wouldn't trade a country lane,
A pasture field of green,
Where skies are blue and cattle graze
In happiness supreme,
A springtime tree that reaches up
A lazy summer breeze,
The new mown hay—a special treat—
The birds' sweet melodies.

I wouldn't trade the rolling hills,
The woods so oft we'd roam,
The little path all snug and safe
That always led to home,
The flowing stream, so clear and bright,
The smell of country air,
The violets and the buttercups
That grew so lovely there.

I wouldn't trade the friendly folks,
The fireside warm and gay,
The orchards laden down with fruit
Upon an autumn day,
The nesting birds at spring's first sign,
The evening's quiet bliss,
The world that God created here
In love and happiness.

There's so much in a country home:
Contentment—peace—and love,
And every tree and mountaintop
Looks up to God above,
Beneath the sun and summer sky
One moment in the shade,
Because they live within my heart
These joys—I wouldn't trade.

East Corinth, Vermont
Fred M. Dole Productions

SUMMER SANCTUARY

Milly Walton

Deep in the heart of the forest
When summer has pierced its gloom
Like sun through a stained-glass window,
There's a vast cathedral room.

The choir of feathered songsters
Warble praise from every aisle,
And he who makes the pilgrimage
May look up and glimpse God's smile.

Mountain Laurel
Norfolk, Connecticut
Dick Smith, Photography

Photo Overleaf
The Grand Tetons
Jackson Hole, Wyoming
Ed Cooper Photo

MEADOW MUSIC

Garnett Ann Schultz

I hear the meadow singing
It finds the world complete,
Across the valley drifts the mist
Into the heavens sweet,
Where green leaves meet the blue of sky—
The mountainside so fair—
I hear frogs piping in the marshes
Upon the summer air.

I held the meadow music
So closely to my heart,
The golden sunlight lit the world
Such beauty to impart.
All outdoor life about me,
The bird notes—joyful sound,
The meadow shared her music
With God's world all around.

Poppies, Coreopsis, and Silver King Artemesia
in a Pennsylvania Meadow
Lefever/Grushow from
Grant Heilman Photography, Inc.

Hairstreak Butterfly
on Pink Zinnia
Ina Mackey

BUTTERFLIES

Ann Thompson Jester

Butterflies are pretty things,
Lifted high on airy wings.
Fluttering, soaring easily,
They seem not to notice me.

Abundantly they seem to spawn
In the day's ecstatic dawn.
Everywhere I look, I see
Winged bits of poetry.

Angle Wing Butterfly
on Orange Zinnia
Ina Mackey

GARDEN VISITORS

Mamie Ozburn Odum

My flower garden was beautiful
With winged colors flying by,
They danced, dipped, and pivoted,
I did not question why.

And every blossom knew them,
Gold, specked, silver, red,
They visited quite gaily
Each blooming flower bed.

They danced like little fairies,
Such grace no one denies,
They were our yearly visitors—
Our summer butterlifes.

11

BITS & PIECES

Let our object be our country, our whole country, and nothing but our country. And, by the blessing of God, may that country itself become a vast and splendid monument, not of oppression and terror, but of wisdom, of peace, and of liberty, upon which the world may gaze with admiration forever.

Daniel Webster

In those vernal seasons of the year when the air is calm and pleasant, it were an injury and sullenness against nature not to go out and see her riches, and partake in her rejoicing with heaven and earth.

Milton

12

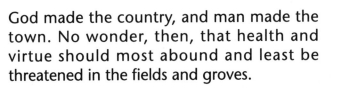

God made the country, and man made the town. No wonder, then, that health and virtue should most abound and least be threatened in the fields and groves.

Cowper

The country is both the philosopher's garden and his library, in which he reads and contemplates the power, wisdom, and goodness of God.

William Penn

Be just and fear not; let all the ends thou aimest at, be thy country's, thy God's, and truth's.

William Shakespeare

When I would beget content and increase confidence in the power and wisdom and providence of Almighty God, I will walk the meadows by some gliding stream, and there contemplate the lilies that take no care, and those very many other little creatures that are not only created, but fed by the goodness of the God of Nature—and therefore must trust in him.

Izaak Walton

Photo Overleaf
Bogie Farm
Peacham, Vermont
Dick Dietrich Photography

GOD'S HELPER

Roy Z. Kemp

A farmer plows his fields with hope,
And plants his seed with care,
And prays for rain as well as sun:
For warm, crop-growing air.

He tends his crops with patient skill
From dawn till time for bed;
He knows God smiles upon his work—
A world waits to be fed.

Photo Opposite
Pioneer Peak from Matanuska Valley
Near Palmer, Alaska
Jeff Gnass Photography

YELLOW GLOW OF SUMMER

Elisabeth Weaver Winstead

Yellow is the color
Of bright finches flying high
And sunflowers with their faces
Tilting upward to the sky.

Yellow is the color
Of the baby's silken hair,
And the sunlight beams that linger
In each shining smile so fair.

Smooth yellow are the apricots
That ripen in warm July,
And tempting, fragrant, yellow quince
Baked in a fresh fruit pie.

Yellow is the firefly's glint
And the butterfly's radiant hue.
Summer sparkles in yellow splendor
As the shimmering sun glows through.

FROM MY G·A·R·D·E·N JOURNAL

Deana Deck

STRAWBERRY (FRAGARIA CHILOENSIS) BLUEBERRY (VACCINIUM) BLACKBERRY (RUBUS EBONY KING)

A Berry Tasty Garden

A bowl of fresh-picked raspberries in a puddle of cream may be the ultimate summer breakfast. That is, unless you prefer blueberry pancakes, sprinkled with powdered sugar and an extra handful of plump, juicy berries. Then there are those delectable summer deserts that with only the slightest rationalization can double as a fruity breakfast: blackberry cobbler, for example, or strawberry shortcake. Or perhaps just a handful of grapes, plucked off the vine on an early morning stroll through the garden.

All it takes to turn this fantasy into reality is a sunny patch of garden soil. Even a south-facing patio or balcony will do. Small fruits are easier for the home gardener today than ever before, thanks to the diligent work being done in plant laboratories and experimental agriculture stations all over the country.

Dwarf fruit trees are one benefit of all this research, enabling even an apartment dweller to grow a containerized small peach or apple tree that will produce full-sized fruit. A major breakthrough has been the discovery of ways to breed disease resistance into otherwise difficult-to-grow fruits. Another development has been the breeding of plants with longer seasons of fruit production with plants that produce more than one crop in a single season. The everbearing strawberry is a good example. It has two fruit producing seasons, spring and fall. These are one of the best choices for those with only a patio or balcony available for gardening, because strawberries are shallow-rooted and do well in vertically arranged tiers or in "strawberry barrels."

During the first growing season, all the blossoms should be picked off the plants. For the June-bearing varieties, this means no berries at all in the first year, but if blooms are pinched off the everbearing varieties until June, a late summer crop will still be produced and the plants will bear more abundantly in the future.

Breeders have also scored some notable victories with the blackberry. Nearly everyone who ever suffered scratched arms and legs picking ripe blackberries on a hot summer day associates their harvesttime with the Fourth of July. Blackberries in the wild still reach their peak of ripeness around this holiday, but today berry season can begin as early as June and extend until nearly Labor Day, thanks to the development of early, mid-season, and late-blooming varieties.

An even greater breakthrough is the development of the thornless blackberry. Not only does it make picking a breeze, it also greatly simplifies pruning. If you don't prune you'll end up with a mass of foliage and fewer berries each year, so anything that makes it easier is valuable. I have a four-year-old Dirkson thornless blackberry patch that produces fruit from late June well into the end of July. The berries are large, sweet, and succulent, and the canes produce so heavily that finding time to harvest and preserve them all is a real challenge. My friends know that they can count on sampling blackberry cobbler anytime they stop by in mid-summer. Since propagating from suckers is easy, I often send them home

with enough small miniature plants to start their own patch. These also mature thorn-free.

The blueberry is another easy-to-grow plant. It not only provides delicious fruit for the table, but doubles as an attractive landscape shrub as well. Many landscapers have begun including blueberry shrubs in their designs because, as ornamentals, they provide garden color almost all year.

In spring, the blueberry shrub is covered with white blossoms with just a tinge of pink. Then come the berries, almost more than one can handle, which are pale blue-white at the start and then turn dark blue. In the fall, the leaves turn yellow as the days grow shorter, and when the cold weather hits, they turn bright crimson. If it is not too windy, the plant can hold its leaves all winter. Blueberries can be grown on a balcony if there is enough space for two half whiskey barrels.

Blueberries have to cross pollinate to produce fruit, so be sure to buy at least two different varieties, and be sure the plants are those that bloom at the same time.

All berry-producing plants require full sun and richly organic, well-drained soil. The blueberry is more demanding than others, requiring in addition a highly acid soil with a pH factor of 4.5 to 5.1. (Most plants are happy at 6.5.) This doesn't present a problem if you have just a few plants or if they are containerized, because you have more control over the soil. If you can grow azaleas or rhododendrons, your soil will suit the blueberries. If you are too far north for these shrubs however, you'll just have to have a soil sample taken to determine the level of acidity and amend accordingly.

Since most fruits do best when planted in early fall, you can still get them into the ground for a head start on next year's crop if you order the plants now. Try your local garden center first, because most mail order nurseries will not ship until the plants are dormant.

_____

Deana Deck's garden column is a regular feature in the Tennessean. *She grows her summer berries in Nashville, Tennessee.*

My Country Homeplace

Elisabeth Weaver Winstead

Give me sweet hay barns
And windswept hollows,
White rumpled clouds laced
With the flight of swallows.

Give me fields of tall corn
In waving green rows,
And the bright orange pumpkins
That harvesttime knows.

Give me rippling creek water
Where children splash and wade
With stately oak trees lending
Cool intervals of shade.

Give me bright meadow daisies
On rolling green hills
And fruit pies cooling
On wide windowsills.

Give me these summer miracles
In treasured beauty traced,
Where life's delights await me
In my country homeplace.

Photo Opposite
Rural Homestead
Near Marxville, Wisconsin
Ken Dequaine Photography

The Farmer

Edna Jaques

He found his joy in common things,
    He ate the royal bread of kings;
His birthright was a quiet soul,
    A healthy body clean and whole.
A battered hat of straw his crown,
    His kingdom was a field of brown.

And there within his fair domain
    He held the scepter of his reign,
The seasons served him bed and board,
    The sun and rain his overlord,
The germ of life in seed and flower
    The living symbols of his power.

He tilled the soil its wealth to find,
    His field, the servant of mankind;
He felt the pulse of nature's blood,
    And spoke the tongue she understood.
He dwelt in bondage fast, yet he
    Was monarch of his destiny.

TRAVELER'S *Diary*

Marian H. Tidwell

SS *Ticonderoga* and Colchester Lighthouse.

One of the brochures given to visitors at Vermont's Shelburne Museum begins with the words "Electra Havemeyer Webb had a vision." Opened in 1947, and dedicated to displaying the ingenuity and craftsmanship of the American people, the museum is the realization of that vision. Its thirty-seven historic buildings, spread over forty-five acres of Vermont countryside, house Mrs. Webb's collection of more than 200,000 pieces of folk art—artifacts from two centuries of American life.

Electra Havemeyer Webb probably inherited her love of collecting from her parents. But while Mr. and Mrs. Havemeyer sought after European fine art, their daughter had an eye for things truly American. Her collections include decoys, paintings, carousel animals, weather vanes, furniture, sleds, carriages, and other items gathered from around the country. And Mrs. Webb did not limit herself to small collectibles; her vision also encompassed American architecture: houses, barns, lighthouses, and boats are all included on the grounds of the Shelburne Museum.

A visit to Shelburne begins with an audiovisual presentation on the history of the creation of the museum in the Passumpsic Round Barn. The barn itself, like most of the museum's structures, is more than merely functional. Originally built in East Passumpsic, Vermont, at the turn of the century in the round design devised by the Shakers, the barn is now home to a collection of antique New England farm tools and vehicles.

After the introductory slide show, visitors are free to walk about the grounds, or to take advantage of the transportation provided by the museum. Among the sights is a covered bridge that Mrs. Webb brought to the museum from the nearby Lamoille River. Once a common sight in the New England landscape, this is now Vermont's only remaining two-lane covered bridge with adjoining footpath. For those with more domestic

Vermont's last remaining two-lane covered bridge with footpath.

interests, there is the Stencil House. Originally built in New York State, the house contains antiques from the first quarter of the nineteenth century, including the original detailed stencilling on its wide-board walls.

The paddle boat SS *Ticonderoga* also has found new life at the Shelburne Museum. Here, on dry land, the ship reminds visitors of an earlier time when transportation was more than simply a means of getting from one place to another. Built in 1906 in the Shelburne port on Lake Champlain, the *Ticonderoga* transported passengers across the lake to New York until more efficient means of travel left it idle. Mrs. Webb recognized the ship's value and arranged for it to be moved inland. The *Ticonderoga* is now the last vertical beam side-wheel steamship intact in the United States and is recognized as a National Historic Landmark.

Of course, there are also the more traditional museum items; the Shelburne has a wonderful collection of American paintings, including works by Audubon, Whistler, Grandma Moses, and Homer, as well as over 350 Currier and Ives lithographs.

The parlor of the Shelburne Museum's Stencil House, with original stencilled walls.

In a building that was once part of the Shelburne Town Hall, visitors will find a collection of American-made quilts. This is perhaps the most fascinating of the museum's many collections. Patchwork quilt tops are the product of the resourceful early American settlers, who saved and tucked away every scrap that might someday be put to use. In the collection at the Shelburne Museum, quilt lovers can read some of the history behind each quilt in the pieced and

Quilt display, Shelburne Museum.

appliqued tops: pineapples stand for hospitality, hearts for brides, cornucopias for abundance, oak leaves for continuing life.

The earliest of the quilts have hand-woven linen or cotton backings, and as batting between the outer layers, many have combed raw cotton, sometimes still containing seeds. Several quilts are patriotic in theme, such as the "Star Spangled Banner," created in 1840. Made up of five pieced stars with a border of stripes and four high-relief stuffed eagles, this quilt features stitched phrases from Francis Scott Key's anthem. Another quilt, pieced together by a Civil War veteran recuperating from his war experiences, contains a fascinating historical record. A combination of pieced work and appliques—including infantrymen and foot soldiers, a woman with a serving tray, doves, oak leaves, and hearts— this "Civil War Counterpane," tells one soldier's tale of the experience of war and of a love found in its aftermath.

The Shelburne Museum has a building, or a collection, for nearly every interest. Tools and trades, textiles, painting, transportation, architecture—if it is a part of American life, it is a part of this fascinating museum. Mrs. Webb's vision lives on in Shelburne, and the artifacts that she assembled become more valuable as time passes and our folk art—a concrete record of our past—begins to disappear. Located in the heart of one of our country's most beautiful natural settings, the museum is truly a remarkable place. To the north is the city of Burlington; to the west, Lake Champlain; to the east, the Green Mountains, and all around, the Vermont countryside. The Shelburne Museum is the perfect center for a fascinating trip back into America's past.

Marian H. Tidwell is a freelance writer in Johnson City, Tennessee.

Photos by Ken Burris, Shelburne Museum,
Courtesy of the Shelburne Museum, Shelburne, Vermont

THE CLOCK TOWER

Donald G. Smith

A thing to be said for the architecture of earlier generations is that it made allowances for clocks. In every town there was a building with a tower, and on every tower was a clock. City halls, railroad stations, banks, libraries, even hotels—they all had clock towers. Where I grew up it was the newspaper building that displayed the distinctive black and white face with Roman numerals and large, stately, steel hands.

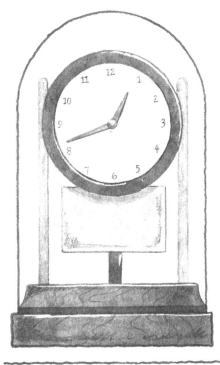

The best thing about these clocks was their system of bells and chimes, sounding once on the half hour and then pealing out an exact count as each new hour began. Time was not simply a system of measurement to those clock tower architects, it was an event. When three o'clock rolled around, it announced itself definitively with three loud bongs. A new hour seemed to hold more promise when declared in this manner, more so than when revealed by a glance at one of today's digital clocks as it softly beeps in the new hour.

In the home families had impressive clocks on their mantelpieces. These too had some special chime to mark the hours. In many homes, clocks were the center of a room's decor and, like the great clock towers, their place of honor gave the passing hours a dignity that is missing from today's electronic time.

I don't like digital watches. These are the products of computerized minds—they exist as measuring devices and nothing more. The same is true of the digital message boards that hang in front of banks in almost every city and town in America. True, they give us the time,

but they do it in such a perfunctory manner. Our obsession with these digital instruments provides a clue to what ails our society today—if we often see the world as cold and indifferent, perhaps it is partly because we wear measuring instruments on our wrists and we read the time from illuminated red or green numbers that peer from little black holes with a precision and consistency that turns the passage of time into merely another business deal, something that we acknowledge and accept, but not anything that touches us personally.

There was once something warm, almost human, about time. Chimes and decorative dial faces gave our timepieces an individuality and charm. Those great old clock towers had a unifying effect upon people; their sound existed to be shared by the community. People anticipated those pealing sounds, they responded to them, and planned their lives around them.

Many cities are now making plans to revitalize their downtown areas. I suggest that any such plans start with a clock tower, one that features four big white round faces, one facing each direction. And the numbers should be black Roman numerals—no dashes or circles—and the hands must be black, too, with rounded arrow points at the ends. And, of course, there must be chimes. Not an anemic buzz or a quick ring within accepted decibel levels, but loud, thunderous, echoing chimes that will ring through the town with dignity and majesty, announcing not only the time, but the unified identity of the town itself. You just don't get that when you hang a digital board in front of the savings and loan company.

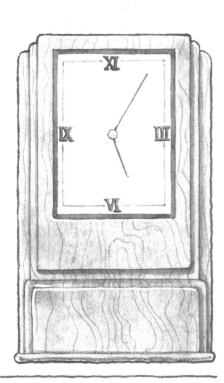

CRAFTWORKS

Necktie Throw Pillows

After my dad passed away I inherited his collection of neckties and decided to make something with them for my family. My daughter suggested a throw pillow; I cut a pattern on a piece of cardboard, started cutting ties, and eventually made pillows for each of my four children and my seven brothers and sisters. The pillows are simple to make and, when made from the ties of a family member, they become priceless heirlooms.

Materials Needed:
- 1 14-inch pillow form
- 2 yds. unbleached domestic or broadcloth
-     Several old neckties
-     Cardboard form (design at right)

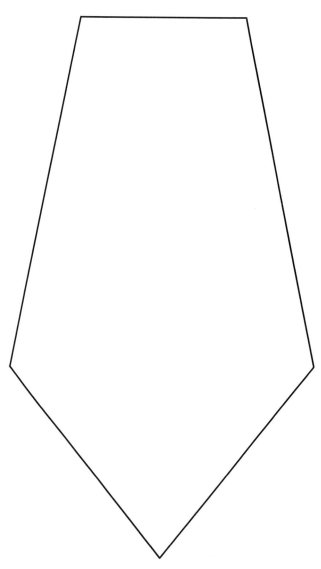

Step One: Making Pillow Top
Cut 2 14-inch squares from material. Cut one round center piece, 3 inches in diameter, and pin to center of one square piece. Cut 6 inches off the large end of the neckties, using cardboard form as guide. By hand, sew the tie pieces to the 14-inch square of material, side by side in a circular pattern around the center piece. Turn ¼-inch seam around the center piece and sew by hand over the unfinished center edges of the neckties.

Step Two: Finishing the Pillow
Make a ruffle by cutting one strip of material, 4 inches wide and 72 inches long. Hem one side by machine. Baste the other side and gather to fit around pillow top.

Step Three: Finishing the Pillow
Baste the right side of the ruffle between the right side of the pillow top and the other 14-inch square of material. Sew, leaving one side unstitched. Trim corners, turn right-side-out, and insert pillow form. Sew final side seam.

Billie Gatlin lives in Brentwood, Tennessee with her husband, whose tie collection she plans to put to use on pillows for her four children and seven grandchildren.

30

The Star-Spangled Banner

Francis Scott Key

O say, can you see, by the dawn's early light,
What so proudly we hailed at the twilight's last gleaming—
Whose broad stripes and bright stars, through the perilous fight,
O'er the ramparts we watched were so gallantly streaming!
And the rocket's red glare, the bombs bursting in air,
Gave proof through the night that our flag was still there;
O say does that star-spangled banner yet wave
O'er the land of the free, and the home of the brave?

On that shore dimly seen through the mists of the deep,
Where the foe's haughty host in dread silences reposes,
What is that which the breeze, o'er the towering steep,
As it fitfully blows, now conceals, now discloses?

Now it catches the gleam of the morning's first beam,
In full glory reflected now shines on the stream;
'Tis the star-spangled banner; O long may it wave
O'er the land of the free, and the home of the brave!

And where is that band who so vauntingly swore
That the havoc of war and the battle's confusion
A home and a country should leave us no more?
Their blood has washed out their foul footsteps's pollution.
No refuge could save the hireling and slave
From the terror of flight, or the gloom of the grave;
And the star-spangled banner in triumph doth wave
O'er the land of the free, and the home of the brave.

O thus be it forever, when free men shall stand
Between their loved homes and war's desolation!
Blest with victory and peace, may the heav'n-rescued land
Praise the power that hath made and preserved us a nation.
Then conquer we must, when our cause it is just,
And this be our motto—"In God is our trust;"
And the star-spangled banner in triumph shall wave
O'er the land of the free, and the home of the brave.

STRAWBERRY TIME

What a delight when the first juicy strawberries begin to ripen—strawberry season is well worth the wait! With their brilliant color and glorious flavor, strawberries are a natural for dessert. We offer you a classic, irresistible recipe to please strawberry lovers everywhere—an old-fashioned shortcake.

COUNTRY STRAWBERRY SHORTCAKE

1/2	cup butter or margarine, softened
1 1/2	cups powdered sugar
2	eggs
1/2	teaspoon grated orange peel
1/2	teaspoon vanilla
1 1/2	cups flour
2	teaspoons baking powder
1/4	teaspoon salt
1/2	cup water
	whipped cream (recipe follows)
1	quart fresh strawberries, stemmed, halved, and tossed with 1/2 cup sugar

Grease and flour 8-inch layer cake pan. In large mixer bowl, cream butter. Gradually add powdered sugar, mixing until blended. Add eggs, orange peel, and vanilla; beat well. Beat in dry ingredients alternately with water. Spoon batter into prepared pan. Bake in 350° oven for 30 minutes or until pick inserted into center comes out clean. Cool 5 minutes. Turn out onto rack to cool completely. Slice cake horizontally into two layers. Place layer on serving plate. Spread with half of the whipped cream. Top with second cake layer. Spoon remaining whipped cream over top of cake; garnish with strawberries. Cut into wedges. Serve remaining berries separately.

Whipped Cream

1	cup heavy cream
3	tablespoons sugar
1/2	teaspoon vanilla

Place cream into chilled bowl. Beat with sugar and vanilla until it forms soft peaks.

Bonnie Aeschliman is a teacher of occupational home economics and a freelance food consultant. She lives in Wichita, Kansas, with her husband and their two children.

Photo courtesy of California Strawberry Advisory Board.

Pamela Kennedy

I ndependence Day is about a lot more than freedom from Mother England. For me, it has as much to do with my freedom to be young again, to do silly things, and to enjoy simple pleasures. It has to do with remembering a time when I couldn't see moon dust up close, or fly faster than the speed of sound, or have a computer for a friend. In short, I can be a kid again on the 4th of July!

At first I thought this was a personal discovery, but over the years I have learned that it is not. People all over the country love to drop the mantle of sophistication and get down to serious silliness on the 4th.

One hot July 4th, in an upscale suburb north of Chicago, I sat on a curb and watched the "World Famous (so they said) Precision Mower Drill Team." Twenty men, dressed in trench coats and fedoras, marched in five columns of four, each pushing a power lawn mower. It was a deafening chorus of Black and Deckers, Snappers, and Craftsmen executing fancy maneuvers up Main Street. Bankers, lawyers, and doctors, mind you, mowing asphalt in eighty-degree weather, grinning like kids out of school—only on the 4th of July.

East of Milwaukee on another Independence Day, we turned out curbside to witness "The Largest (they claimed) Kazoo Marching Band in the Entire U.S. of A." One-hundred-fifty folks marched past in Groucho glasses, complete with oversized nose and mustache, belting out a nasal version of "Stars and Stripes Forever." I'll bet you couldn't persuade even one of those people to walk a block playing the kazoo on any other day of the year. But on the 4th of July, the ridiculous becomes sublime.

This thought returned to me at our most recent neighborhood 4th of July extravaganza. Early in the day we gathered at the community pool to witness feats of skill and agility. The crazy dive and big splash contests were great fun, but the fans went wild at the greased watermelon race. Two teams battled valiantly to win in a contest based loosely on water polo. The big difference was, of course, the ball—in this case a ten pound watermelon coated with Crisco. I hadn't imagined that folks could get so wrought up over a piece of slippery fruit, but there were cheers, jeers, and just plain hilarity when the "Vegematics" finally squirted the melon to victory!

We hardly had time to catch our breath before the fire truck arrived to take interested parties for a ride. No matter if you are over forty, climb up and make the siren go! Some of us had waited decades for the thrill of this moment. Any other day we might have deferred to a child, but on the 4th of July, the child in each of us would not be denied!

There were over-done burgers and charcoal-striped hot dogs for supper, with corn on the cob, and thick, drippy slices of watermelon. Naval officers who at other times dined with admirals and ambassadors licked their sticky fingers and then lined up for an impromptu seed spitting contest. The victor got to pick first when we chose sides for the annual tug-of-war.

As the sun began to set, the tugging teams positioned themselves. Tension mounted, the rope stretched taut over a great puddle of mud, and at the signal, the pulling began. Traditionalists favored the organized chant and pull technique, while the avant-garde contingent screamed like banshees and dashed back and forth, throwing off the timing of the opposition. I don't remember who won, but there were plenty of muddy bodies when the competition ended. There were also plenty of accusations about cheating and squashed toes. Shortly, things degenerated into a good-natured, mud-slinging free-for-all. (You know, the kind of thing your mother would never let you do when you were a kid!)

As darkness fell we gathered—muddy, sweaty, tired, and stuffed—to watch the fireworks. Children's wonder filled us again as the multi-colored star showers exploded in the sky. I held hands with my middle-aged, mud-caked husband. Tomorrow, we would be businesslike and grown up again: neat, tidy, and responsible. But tonight, under the star-spangled sky, we were kids once more. Tonight it was the 4th of July!

Pamela Kennedy is a freelance writer of short stories, articles, essays, and children's books. Married to a naval officer and mother of three children, she has made her home on both U.S. coasts and currently resides in Hawaii. She draws her material from her own experiences and memories, adding bits of imagination to create a story or mood.

Child's Play

We're Very Good Friends, My Father and I

P.K. Hallinan

We're very good friends,
My father and I.
We like to play catch
And watch trains roar by.
And sometimes we'll sit
At the base of a tree
And talk about places
We wish we could see.
Or sometimes we'll walk
And we won't say a word.
But that's okay too,
For good friends to do.

We like to play sports,
My father and I,
Like tennis and horseshoes
And fishing with flies.
In winter we'll go
For a romp in the snow!
In summer we'll play
At the beach the whole day!
But then there are times
That we just sit and stare
At far distant stars
That light the night air.
We really like stars,
My father and I.

And always we're happy
Just being together
Like clams in the sand
Or birds of a feather.
We like to go camping,

And we like to play cards.
We even like mowing
and hoeing the yard.
But once in a while,
We'll just take a drive
And feel all the gladness
Of being alive.
We always have fun,
My father and I.

Then in the evening
We usually stand
Alone in the kitchen
And talk man to man.
And I see in his eyes
How deeply he cares,
And I hear in his voice
All the feelings he bears.

My father's my teacher;
He's my leader, my guide.
And I like being with him,
Right there at his side.
He's helped me to grow
And to stand very tall.
And I know in my heart
He's the best dad of all!

So I guess in the end,
Love's the best reason why…
We're very good friends,
My father and I!

Under Daddy's Wing

Carol Shaw Johnston

My children are so conditioned to wearing seatbelts that if I happen to start the car before they are fully buckled in, they will tell me to wait. During my own childhood, however, cars did not have seatbelts, and it never occurred to us to want them.

My family regularly made long car trips to visit my grandparents. In the front seat, my father would drive and my mother would hold my younger brother. In the back seat, my older brother, my four sisters, and I would crowd into every available bit of space. I remember jockeying for preferred positions; window seats were popular, and not just because of the scenic opportunities—carsickness was a regular occurrence, and it had a domino effect.

Those of us sitting next to the windows, with a ready supply of fresh air, were least likely to fall victim to that particular malady. The back window ledge was another popular spot. I spent many an hour curved into that ledge, gazing up at the stars through the window and dreaming the miles away.

However, each time that I climbed into the car I eagerly anticipated an invitation from my father to sit in the most treasured seat of all: "Come sit under my wing, Cabbie," he would call to me. The invitation meant I could sit by his side, with his arm held out in front of me, elbow bent like a wing to keep me safe. As a little girl growing up in a large family, I never experienced a more secure feeling than when I

40

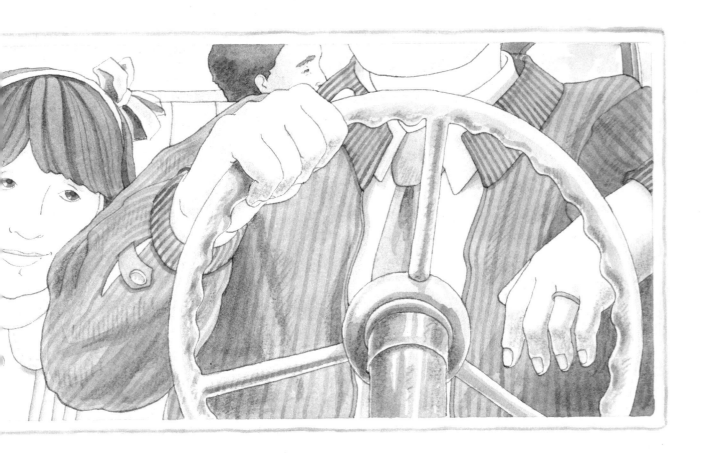

was snuggled close to my father, enjoying his warmth and attention as we traveled down the highway.

We children would always ask Daddy to tell us a story. He loved to tell us about his childhood adventures, like the time he and his younger brother went skinny-dipping in a nearby river and got caught in a sudden rainstorm. The river turned into a churning whirlpool in a matter of minutes. Daddy had to pull his brother out of the river, and then they scrambled to where their clothes had been hung on two small bushes, about fifty feet apart. Suddenly there was a crash of lightning and a giant tree fell right between the two shivering boys. We children would sit in the quiet, dark car and listen, and in our imaginations, we could see the swirling water, feel the sharp bite of the driving rain, hear the heart-stopping thunder, and then when he finished, we would almost cry with relief to realize how close Daddy had come to death. That story was only one of a long list of boyhood tales, and we knew them all by heart. Each time I sat under Daddy's wing, I requested my own favorite.

My father was a fair man, though, so my turn came only occasionally. And even after my three older siblings became too old to sit next to him, I still had to compete with three younger ones. But having to wait my turn made it seem all the more special when my chance did finally come.

But, as children do, we grew up, and soon we were all too old, and those memories were relegated to family history books.

Now I am thankful that my own children automatically fasten their own seatbelts; that is the only truly safe way to travel. I am also thankful, though, that in my own childhood I was able to experience the loving security of sitting under Daddy's wing.

Letter to Father

Dear Father, I want you to know
You've always been more than a parent to me.
You've always been my guiding light,
Ever since I played 'round your knee.

I've followed you to the barber shop,
You've carried me to the store.
You've built a bed for my dolly,
I can vision it now on the floor.

Together we went to the circus,
We watched the horses race down the track,
And many a fine parade I have seen
While perched high on my Daddy's back.

From infancy to womanhood,
You've been my dearest friend;
To offer thanks seems oh so small,
But I've oceans of love to send.

And could I achieve but one aim in life,
My greatest desire would be
To be the kind of parent
That you have been to me.

Gladys Manes Kidwell
Cleveland, Tennesse

To You, Father

Once again it's Father's Day,
When fathers reign supreme;
My heart is filled with happiness,
For Dad, to me you're king.

In my eyes you're ten feet tall,
There's nothing you can't do,
The many gifts you gave to me,
I'll use my whole life through.

Oh yes, you gave me many things,
Gifts I cannot measure,
But most of all you gave me love—
God's most precious treasure.

Julie E. Jones
Lexington, Kentucky

Editor's Note: Readers are invited to submit unpublished, original poetry, short anecdotes, and humorous reflections on life for possible publication in future *Ideals* issues. Please send copies only; manuscripts will not be returned. Writers receive $10 for each published submission. Send material to "Readers' Reflections," Ideals Publishing Corporation, P.O. Box 140300, Nashville, Tennessee, 37214-0300

Reflections

Who is a Father?

A father is someone who reads difficult blueprints but has a hard time deciphering the instruction sheet for a backyard swing set.

A father is someone who is a great fix-it-man, but who needs Mom to find the screwdriver before he can fix anything.

A father is someone who gets tears in his eyes at his little girl's wedding.

A father is someone who doesn't watch his son back out of the driveway in his new car.

A father is someone who doesn't keep a tally sheet of what he spends on ice cream, bubble gum, birthday presents, gym shoes, or lost mittens.

A father is someone who on his day off can be found playing with the kids, mowing the lawn, or walking miles at the zoo.

A father is someone to hold you up if you can't see the parade going by.

And, above all, a father is a man who works daily for his family, knowing all the while that his only reward will be a hug, a kiss, or just a "Hi Daddy" at the end of the day.

Evelyn Heinz
McHenry, Illinois

A SLICE OF LIFE

Edgar A. Guest

DADDIES

I would rather be the daddy
    Of a romping, roguish crew,
Of a bright-eyed chubbie laddie
    And a little girl of two,
Than the monarch of a nation,
    In his high and lofty seat,
Taking empty adoration
    From the subjects at his feet.

I would rather own their kisses,
    As at night to me they run,
Than to be the king who misses
    All the simpler forms of fun.
When his dreary day is ending
    He is dismally alone,
But when my sun is descending
    There are joys for me to own.

He may ride to horns and drumming;
    I must walk a quiet street,
But when once they see me coming,
    Then on joyous, flying feet
They come racing to me madly
    And I catch them with a swing,
And I say it proudly, gladly,
    That I'm happier than a king.

You may talk of lofty places;
    You may boast of pomp and power;
Men may turn their eager faces
    To the glory of an hour,
But give me the humble station
    With its joys that long survive,
For the daddies of the nation
    Are the happiest men alive.

Edgar A. Guest began his career in 1895 at the age of fourteen when his work first appeared in the Detroit Free Press. *His column was syndicated in over 300 newspapers, and he became known as "The Poet of the People."*

Country Child

C.H. Channing

Farmhouse born,
Quiet and mild,
Flower-laden
Country child,
Simple in your way of living—
Looking, finding,
Sharing, giving.
Bird songs in the early morn,
Haying time
When you were born;
Wade the brooks,
Inquire of shadows,
Climb the trees,
Enjoy the meadows,
And pumpkin pies,
And bales of hay,
Stay the way you are today—
Though the world
Grow rough and wild,
Stay soft-patterned—
Country child.

Golden Memories

Barbara L. Freund

The sweet, intoxicating smell of honey-suckle on a trellis and the soft chirping of crickets remind me of cool summer evenings with my family on our front porch.

Just after dinner—right before darkness settled—we would relax in the bright red and blue chairs; the cool metal against my skin sent goose bumps up and down my arms and legs.

The grownups would discuss the events of the day or the weather. My brother and I talked of the new children on the corner of Beacon Street, or how many days it would take to finish the neighborhood clubhouse in the Dawson's back yard, or which baseball cards we needed to complete that year's set.

Blondie, our fat old dog, would lie on the top step as if guarding us from intruders, but in truth, she was too old and too tired to do anything about them if they came. An occasional thump of her tail told us she was content.

Sitting on the bottom step leisurely washing, Perky, the slinky yellow-striped cat, was preparing for his nightly prowl around the neighborhood.

As the shadows lengthened, we went searching in the garage for a jar to catch fire-

flies. Then we would creep along the thick hedge in the backyard and gently grasp the twinkling insects out of the air.

When our jars were crawling with fireflies, we would return to the front steps, take off the lid, and watch them scramble out, blinking their yellow-green lights as they flew away in the early darkness. We watched in awe, wondering how they could make their eerie little lights without electricity.

As darkness deepened, the moths and millers began their nightly ritual of beating their wings against the screen door, frantically swarming to the light, attracted by some strong mysterious inner force.

Soon the street lights made their little islands of light along the curb. At this time, the Dawson boys always arrived for our nightly game of "Hide and Seek" in our dark, shadowy backyard. My favorite place to hide was behind the thick patch of hollyhocks at the edge of the garden.

Afterwards, tired and out of breath, we would rest in the cool, dewy grass looking for stars, marveling at their brightness even across millions of miles.

Finally, Mother would call us in, and after a snack we would tumble into bed. Tired but happy and relaxed, we were ready to dream of tomorrow's fun.

Even now, some thirty years later, those happy golden moments of summer's evenings are etched in my mind and my heart brims with gratitude to my loving family for providing me such a rich and wondrous time to remember.

I Remember a Summer Kitchen

Minnie Klemme

I remember a summer kitchen
With a calendar four feet long,
Where the coal oil lamp made shadows
And the range was iron strong.

I remember yeast loaves baking,
The canning of berries and jell,
Stone jars of dills and cabbage—
The kraut we loved so well.

I remember a summer kitchen
And food for the harvest hands,
For threshing crews and shellers:
The many farm demands.

I remember the food and the largess
That came from its mighty store:
The ever-ready handout—
And always the promise for more.

I remember a summer kitchen,
The blueprints are stored in my heart;
As warm as the range and the kettles,
As bright as the calendar art.

DADDY'S FARM

Lon Myruski

It sits resting in a valley,
Just five miles outside of town.
The red, chipped barn needs painting,
And the silo's falling down.
But still, its character and nature
Can seduce your soul with charm,
It's the place I spent my childhood,
Growing up on Daddy's farm.

I remember catching catfish,
On a lazy afternoon,
While dragonflies lay dreaming,
On the lily pads in bloom.
Skipping flat rocks across the frog pond—

Country fun that caused no harm:
Life was full of simple pleasures,
Living down on Daddy's farm.

There were times, while picking berries,
When I had to quickly snatch
To beat the hungry blackbirds
In the ripe blackberry patch.
And when that big, long locomotive
Blew its whistle-like alarm,
I'd run waving out a welcome
As it passed by Daddy's farm.

Now I walk these fields and meadows,
Harvesting the memories
Grown from roots set back in childhood
That have always guided me.
We worked together in those hayfields,
Day by day, the sun shone on our arms
Like a badge of honest labor—
Life was good on Daddy's farm.

COLLECTOR'S CORNER

Butter Molds

Although historians do not know when people first made butter, they do know that in India, butter was churned from water buffalo milk as early as 2000 B.C. Advancements in butter production were slow, and it wasn't until 1859, in New York, that the first creamery to produce large quantities of butter by machine was opened. Consequently, throughout our country's early history and until the beginning of the 1900s, most rural families continued to do their own butter churning.

The custom of decorating butter originated in Europe in the 1600s and was carried over to the American colonies. Churning butter was usually the chore of a farmer's wife. She sold her homemade butter at a weekly market in town and used her own special stamp or mold to identify it as hers. Thus, the design not only improved the appearance of the butter, but it became an individual's personal trademark. In the marketplace, this molded and stamped butter was called "print butter" to distinguish it from butter which was marketed in crocks or tubs. Print butter generally brought a higher price, much as name brands do today. As a rule, no two farms within a specified area would use the same design. This led to the development of numerous variations of patterns and designs.

The earliest molds existing today were made in the late 1700s and early 1800s. Most, however, were made between 1840 and 1900. Butter molds were generally made either of pine or poplar, because these woods were easily carved; however, walnut, cherry, and maple were also used.

Butter molds show whittled designs on small wooden plates. Because most molds were made by untutored whittlers, the technique used in making them was "chip carving"—simple cuts and twists made quickly with a sharp knife. The design on both molds and stamps was usually carved so that it produced a raised image on the butter. At first, butter molds did not have handles, but as they developed, handles were added to the plates for easier removal.

Butter molds were either box or cup-shaped and were made in various sizes: pounds, halves, quarters, and eighths. Some were even made to produce individual pats for use at the table.

Immigrants from different countries brought their own unique designs and motifs. The tulip was predominant in Pennsylvania among German immigrants. British influence was exhibited in the more symmetrical and formal designs—carefully spaced motifs such as fruits and flowers—and well-defined border designs.

Pineapples, sheaves of wheat, hearts, stars, acorns, crescents, eagles, cows, and other barn-yard animals were popular designs. One ambitious mold-maker even carved the words "Good butter. . . Taste it" into his butter mold. The most valuable molds and stamps are those which have animal, bird, or other odd shapes. The most sought-after motifs are the eagle, the cow, the fish, and the rooster.

Records of the use and design of butter molds are scarce. Because they were considered ordinary household items, they were generally taken for granted and their potential value as a collectible was overlooked.

Only recently have collectors begun to recognize the fine examples of folk art which are found in the unique designs of butter molds. However, now that the popularity of butter molds and stamps as collectibles is increasing, they are quickly beginning to disappear from the market.

Carol Shaw Johnston

Carol Shaw Johnston, a public school teacher, writes articles and short stories. She lives with her family in Brentwood, Tennessee.

Country
CHRONICLE
— Lansing Christman —

When June arrives, a farmer's child looks to summer vacation from school, to stepping through the doorway to the open country, to meadows, fields, woodland streams, ponds, and lakes. Even once old enough to work alongside the adults in the field or the garden, summer still means time for the child to meander in solitude through the natural world.

In my grade school days, long ago, in the era of the one-room schoolhouse, I walked a winding dirt road and watched the blossoms appearing along the roadside and in the fields. The white daisies stood like exclamation marks in the green of timothy that covered the flats. We boys, plucking the white petals, would repeat the lines: "She loves me, she loves me not." It was always a disappointment when the last petal proved to be "not."

I learned about birds on those walks to school, the bubbling song of bobolinks in the tall

hay, the whistle of the meadowlark, the "o-ka-lees" of the redwings back in the swale. I listened to the field sparrow's plaintive song; I watched the bluebirds nesting in aging apple trees along the way. Robins and orioles built nests in the roadside trees.

Nature was there at my very side in those early years. It was then I decided I wanted the country to be my home. I wanted my roots in the land; I wanted to be witness to the miraculous beauty of growing things. I wanted to hear the songs of the birds, the purring of the woodland rills, the swish of timothy as it undulated in the June wind, and the rustling of corn and grain.

Even during my forty years at editorial desks in the news world, I lived in the country. Here I have always found my peace and tranquility, for God has walked at my side around every bend of the road of my life.

And here in the country, rich in psalms and scriptures, where I can "lift up mine eyes unto the hills," here I am still at peace.

The author of two published books, Lansing Christman has been contributing to Ideals for almost twenty years. Mr. Christman has also been published in several American, foreign, and braille anthologies. He lives in rural South Carolina.

Rural Fulfillment

Rosaline Guingrich

Here, at the little school, from common clay
Were fashioned vessels of great worth.
Through days when autumn lavished
   on the earth
The gold she hoarded in her copper urn
And bare, brown fields awaited vernal spring;
Through icy months when bitter winds
Bit at feet that waded through drifting snow
Until again the fresh sod yielded to the plow—
Here wrought the potter with great care
That youth, his handiwork, might be
Of greatest service to his countrymen and God.

Photo Opposite
The Old Schoolhouse
near St. Helena, Californi
Ed Cooper Photo

William Holmes McGuffey

Moira Davison Reynolds

H ad you been a school child in the midwest 150 years ago, chances are that you would have used McGuffey's *Readers*, teaching tools developed by William Holmes McGuffey. A child of the western frontier, McGuffey devoted his adult life to improving the education of children in the expanding American West.

Because free public schooling was not available in McGuffey's day, his mother taught him to read using the Bible as her text, and thereafter he provided for his own education, working to earn the money for tutors up until the age of twenty. He then went on to college and studied Hebrew and philosophy as preparation for a career in teaching.

McGuffey became a popular and innovative instructor at Miami University in Oxford, Ohio. Intensely interested in developing reading methods for the young, McGuffey established a private experimental school in his backyard. He was particularly concerned with the teaching of reading and correct pronunciation; this proved to be very significant, as many of the students who would learn from his *Readers* would be German immigrants, new to the sounds of the English language.

McGuffey's interest in literacy naturally included an interest in public education; this, he believed, was the only means by which the United States could ensure the literacy of its citizens. While teaching at Miami University, McGuffey addressed the state legislature of Ohio in support of free public education; his reputation began to spread and, in 1826, Truman and Smith Publishers asked McGuffey to prepare for them a series of reading textbooks — the *Eclectic Readers* — which would include a primer, a speller, and four advanced readers.

The texts were an immediate success. Edition after edition was produced, and when the project outgrew the capabilities of Truman and Smith, other, larger publishers became involved. The *Readers* became the basic texts in 37 states. Only in New England, where they had competition from *Worcester's Readers*, were the McGuffey texts anything but standard schoolroom material. According to one estimate, more than 122 million *Readers* were sold between 1836 and 1920.

Why were these texts so popular? Perhaps it is because they were "western books for western people." Their author was a product of the expanding west, and his original readership was the first-born generation of that frontier. The books were illustrated with scenes and objects from the lives of frontier children, and the sentences were short and simple, with themes familiar to an agrarian population.

On a more subtle plane, the *Readers* set examples of conduct which spoke to the religious beliefs, as well as the practical needs, of American families. Simple, direct lessons were what made the *Readers* so comfortable and so popular:

> All that you do
> Do with your might.
> Things done by halves
> Are not done right.

Children learned to read, while at the same time learning how to live. Horatio Alger-type stories were also common, emphasizing that where there is a will, there is a way — a vital lesson for those devoted to the development of the new nation.

McGuffey believed that even the most basic education must include some knowledge of the classics and of philosophy. He introduced, at appropriate levels, selections from Shakespeare, Hawthorne, Whittier, Tennyson, Thackeray, and others. The more advanced *Readers* contained examples of some of the great oratory of Britain and the United States. Material from Calhoun and Webster, for example, helped instill patriotism. In their day, McGuffey's *Readers* were frequently the only books in homes besides the Bible. Thus, the literary selections often gave readers their first exposure to the great writings of the English language, and in many cases, instilled a love of reading that had not before had the chance to develop.

McGuffey did not end his fight for quality education with the publication of his first *Readers,* rather he continued to work unflaggingly. Not long before his death in 1873, he visited the southern states recovering from the Civil War to speak on the power of public education and the benefits of widespread literacy.

"Train up a child in the way he should go: and when he is old, he will not depart from it" (Prov. 22:6). This Biblical exhortation is a final key to understanding the power of McGuffey's methods. To him, formal education was a basic element of life, entirely necessary to the development of the child. Today, this idea is taken for granted in the United States, but McGuffey, in his day, was a true pioneer. His *Readers* taught generations of Americans, including William Howard Taft, Thomas Edison, Clarence Darrow, Mark Twain, and Henry Ford, and his methods remain at the heart of the American public education system.

LET US GO BACK

Thomas Curtis Clark

Let us go back
To the simpler and better things;
Let us retrace our steps
From our greed-born bickerings
Back to the quietness
Of plain, good friendliness.

Let us go back
To the old roads of beauty's quest;
Let us again find joy
In the fields and the woods, possessed
By the thrill of the spring,
And of summer wandering.

Let us go back
To old-fashioned content, our wealth
Found in the garden nooks,
And beneath home roofs.
Let the health of the trees and the grass
Be ours, as the seasons pass.

LET US GO BACK from the book *HOME ROADS AND FAR HORIZONS* by Thomas Curtis Clark. Copyright © 1935 by Willet, Clark, & Company. Reprinted by permission of Harper & Row, Publishers, Inc.

Congratulations for the new champion. UPI/Bettmann Newsphotos

FARMING:
"Though Dynasties Pass"

Only a man harrowing clods…" wrote Poet Thomas Hardy. "Yet this will go onward the same though Dynasties pass…War's annals will fade…ere their story die."

Across Iowa's rich checkerboard of farm lands, men shucked the last of the hog-fattening corn, shaved the empty yellowed stalks from their fields, plowed the brown earth.

Last week they took time off. Men who work with the earth take pride not only in production but in the way the job is done. On the Henry Keppy farm near Davenport, 125,000 farmers and their families gathered to see how the job was done by the best of them at the annual national cornhusking contest.

As a curtain raiser for the huskers was a plowman's match, an innovation on the program, held on the neighboring Denger farm. The

Crowds gather at the National Cornhusking Championship.   UPI/Bettmann Newsphotos

straightest furrows, the neatest turns with a tractor-drawn plough were made by Fred Timbers, who had traveled from Ontario to show what Canadian farmers could do. Fred Timbers became the first international champion of plowmen.

Next day, 21 local champions from eleven States lined up in the Keppy cornfield to wait the starting bomb in the husking contest. Favored by fence-row experts to win were Marion Link, Iowa State champion, Ecas Vaughan, Illinois State champion, Irving Bauman, also from Illinois, runner-up in the nationals in 1935 and 1938. The contestants, some of them stripped to the waist, sweated up and down the corn rows, snatching off the dried ears, husking them with a hook strapped to the wrist, flinging them against the "bang-boards" of tractor-drawn wagons.

Eighty minutes later time was called. The contestants were panting, splotched with blood from cutting themselves on stiff corn leaves. Judges pawed over the wagonloads, deducted gleanings, weighed the results, announced that Irving Bauman had set a new record of 46.71 bushels, had won the 1940 national championship. Second: Marion Link, whose 46.36 bushels also topped the old record of 41.52.

The 125,000 farmers and their families listened to songs by Indian children from the Sac and Fox reservations, with a slow, critical eye looked over the farm implements on display at the Keppy farm, grinned at a map of Iowa made of over a million corn kernels. But what they really liked best were Irving Bauman's 46.71 bushels of husked corn, Plowman Timbers' neat turns and straight rows.

TIME, November 11, 1940

COUNTRY PRAYER

Craig E. Sathoff

O hear my humble prayer
And bless, dear Lord, I pray,
The myriad threads in nature's cloak
That beautify my day.

I thank you for the lace-leafed birch,
The oak tree straight and tall;
The crimson-painted maple tree,
The golden gowns of fall.

I thank you for the time to plant,
The times of sun and rain,
The time to watch the fruits appear
And harvesttime again.

I thank you for the joy of friends
With whom to love and share,
For days of rest and holiday,
For days with toil to bear.

I thank you for the natural things:
For daisies in the lane,
And berries in the old fence row,
And gentle springtime rain.

O hear my simple country prayer
That from my heart overflows
To thank you for the precious gifts
A country person knows.

Photo Opposite
Indian Paintbrush
The Selkirk Mountains
Glacier National Park, British Columb[
Ed Cooper Photo

66

Roads

Milly Walton

Roads arouse my interest
And I'm eager to explore
Their vanishing silver ribbons,
But paths intrigue me more.

A winding little lane
Where wild birds choose to nest
In the shelter of a thicket
Somehow suits me best.

Along its tranquil way,
Red rambler roses twine,
And every sylvan bend,
Some new delights I find.

Great roads built by man
With power and people teem,
But lanes are left for those
Who seek a place to dream.

Riverside Reveries

Patience Strong

Resting by the riverside,
Life's problems pass away
And fade like mists into the peace
And beauty of the day;
Watching how the swallows skim
With swiftness and with grace,
Where the branches of the willows,
  weeping, interlace.

Noting how the rushes quiver
In the restless breeze,
And how the rays of golden light
Are sifted through the trees;
Lulled into contentment
By the water flowing by
Beneath the lovely ceiling of
  the quiet summer sky.

OTHER DAYS

Douglas Malloch

I want to hear some songs of old
    And feel some old-time things,
Like "Silver Threads Among the Gold,"
    Because it always brings
The calm and peace of other days,
The simple life and quiet ways
    Of years that are no more,
The waiting table, cheery blaze,
    The open cabin door.

I want to see some things of old
    That now I do not see—
I want to see the marigold,
    The shady maple tree,
The grasses that were sweet with dew,
The sun that warmed the heart of you,
    The lily in the pond,
And up above the sky of blue
    That seemed the blue Beyond.

This life is swifter than the old,
    We cannot stop to love—
So much is bought, so much is sold,
    We miss the value of
The things that are not sold or bought,
The gifts that only loving brought,
    The words of honest praise,
The friendly smile, the friendly thought—
    The things of other days.

Country Church

Grace Noll Crowell

Symbols of faith they lift their reaching spires
Above green groves down many a country way,
And on the wide plains there are altar fires
That light the forms of those who kneel to pray.
And I have seen them stand knee-deep in wheat:
White country churches, rising from the sod,
Where men, in gratitude for bread to eat,
Have paused and reared their altars to their God.

Symbols they are to mankind's daily need:
The urgent need to pray, the need to praise.
Without their altars, men grow blind indeed,
And grope, bewildered, down unlighted ways.
The look of God is over every land
Where men have toiled, and where their churches stand.

Photo Opposite
Wonalancet, New Hampshire
Fred Sieb Photography

IN THE COUNTRY

Olive Dunkelburger

When it's twilight in the country
And the evening chores are done,
The lamps of home are lighted
Bringing cheer to everyone.

There is mending to be finished,
There are lessons to be learned,
While the menfolk talk of planting
And tally what was earned.

A bowl of red-cheeked apples
Are the children's only sweets—

Content with just the simple things
To make their lives complete.

There's a warm and homey feeling
When a neighbor's light appears,
Like a beacon in the darkness—
Such a welcome it endears.

Through the peaceful summer evening
Nature tunes her symphony
Of the small creatures' music
While the moon waits patiently.

Though nighttime rest comes early
Grateful thanks are said in part,
For the countless daily blessings
That befall a family's heart.

Readers' Forum

I received my first Ideals *and it brought back such fond memories. When I was eight (I am now forty) my grandmother gave me a Christmas* Ideals *book and I began to carry this book to grade school, junior high, and high school when a short story was needed or a poem for class. Needless to say, after all these years I still have the book, it is held together by tape and staples and there are hand written notes on some of the pages where a presentation was made; what a treat to find out I can still subscribe to your book...Thanks to you, I can now enjoy this book again...*

Sandy Brooks
Independence, Missouri

I've written before about not having a book for June titled Father's Day*...not one of us would be here if not for our dear fathers...credit is due to our fathers as well as our mothers.*

Mary Lee Faulkner
Starke, Florida

Ed: We certainly agree that fathers deserve equal parenting credit with mothers, and we have included a section devoted to fathers in this issue. Although we currently have no plans for an entire Father's Day issue, we appreciate your suggestion and encourage other readers to express their opinions, and to send us poems and stories they have written about their own fathers.

The photo above was sent to us without identification. If you can tell us more about this cat, or if you have a picture of your own pet that you'd like to share with other *Ideals* readers, please send us a snapshot. Selected photos will be published in each issue; no photos can be returned, however, so make sure you've got a duplicate

A friend who has been receiving the Ideals magazine for a number of years gave me the September issue...because of the article "Legendary Americans"...I found this article very interesting and very well-written, emphasizing the friendship between two very dear friends, each admiring the work of the other. I am a niece of Mr. Henry Ford; when I opened the magazine to the page of the article I was surprised to see Edsel Bryant Ford's picture instead of that of my Uncle Henry. Edsel was Clara and Henry Ford's only son...I believe that Ideals would want to know of the error and correct it.

Catherine Ruddiman
Boca Raton, Florida

Ed: Miss Ruddiman is correct. The portrait we published is of Edsel, not Henry, Ford. We regret our error, and we thank all the readers who wrote to bring this mistake to our attention.

In a few days I will be 93 years old, and all through the years I have been reading and enjoying the Ideals magazine. I have yet to see or read a poem that really tickled my funny bone. Your articles and poems are really beautiful, but what really does a person good is to read something that makes you chuckle out loud. Doesn't anyone write anything funny anymore?

Alice Z. Fritz
Friedens, Pennsylvania

* * *

Want to share your crafts?
Readers are invited to submit original craft ideas for possible development and publication in future Ideals issues. Please send query letter (with photograph, if possible) to Editorial Features Department, Ideals Publishing Corporation, P.O. Box 140300, Nashville, Tennessee 37214-0300. Please do not send craft samples; they cannot be returned.

This inquisitive cat belongs to Editorial Assistant Fran Morley. One-year-old Gracie was originally named after Gracie Allen, a favorite comedienne, but Fran has decided that she displays a greater likeness to Hurricane Gracie than to her human namesake. Gracie lives in Hermitage, Tennessee, with Fran and her husband Tom.

GOD'S LINES

Edna Green Hines

I planned to write a poem
In praise of beauty's God;
But oh! I found a poem
Growing from the sod.

Anemones and daisies
And shades of glowing gold,
Orchid-tinted bells were there,
All that the arms could hold.

The waters of the lake I saw
With diamonds sprinkled o'er,
While overhead a white gull sailed—
I needed nothing more.

The poem that I meant to write
Was all around me spread;
No words of mine could add a thing.
Instead, God's lines I read.

God wrote for me a poem,
I loved each phrase and word,
The lapping of the waters,
The song of praising bird.

The cadence of his music,
The beauty of the whole
Was June's sweet benediction—
God's poem filled my soul.